SEVEN FATHERS

RETOLD BY
ASHLEY RAMSDEN

ILLUSTRATIONS BY
ED YOUNG

A NEAL PORTER BOOK · ROARING BROOK PRESS · NEW YORK

To George and Vicki Levenson
—A.R.

Text copyright © 2011 Ashley Ramsden
Illustrations copyright © 2011 by Ed Young
A Neal Porter Book
Published by Roaring Brook Press
Roaring Brook Press is a division of Holtzbrinck Publishing Holdings Limited Partnership
175 Fifth Avenue, New York, New York 10010
www.roaringbrookpress.com

Distributed in Canada by H. B. Fenn and Company Ltd.

Library of Congress Cataloging-in-Publication Data

Ramsden, Ashley.
    Seven fathers / Ashley Ramsden ; illustrated by Ed Young. — 1st ed.
        p. cm.
    "A Neal Porter Book."
    Summary: A lone traveler, tired, hungry, and cold, finds a house and asks for a room for the night,
but the old man to whom he speaks refers him to his father, and that man to his father, until he is
finally rewarded for his efforts by the eldest.
    ISBN 978-1-59643-544-5
    [1. Hospitality—Fiction. 2. Fathers—Fiction. 3. Old age—Fiction. 4. Fairy tales.] I. Young, Ed, ill. II. Title.

PZ7.R1445Sev 2011
[E]—dc22

                                                                        2010009674

Roaring Brook Press books are available for special promotions and premiums.
For details contact: Director of Special Markets, Holtzbrinck Publishers.

First Edition 2011
Book design by Jennifer Browne
Printed in December 2010 in China by Toppan Leefung Printing Ltd., Dongguan City, Guangdong Province
1 3 5 7 9 8 6 4 2

One winter's evening, a lone traveler trudged down a winding forest road looking for a place to spend the night.

The air was frosty, the sky as dark as pitch, and the snow lay deep upon the ground. The traveler had already walked many, many miles, and he knew that unless he found shelter soon, he would have to lie down in the wet, icy snow. On such a cold night, he might never wake again.

Hoping to find a warm place where he could spend the night, he muttered desperately, "Just one more mile. Just one more mile, and then I'm done for."

And scarcely had he gone around the next bend when he saw, off in the distance, a house blazing with lights. "At last," the traveler said. "At last, I've found a place where I can spend the night."

He gathered his last drop of energy, crossed a snow-filled meadow, and made it to the front porch of the house where he found an old man busily chopping wood.

The traveler went up to him and said, "Good evening, Father. I'm so glad I found you. Would you, by any chance, have a room where I could spend the night?"

"Oh," said the old man, "I'm not the father of the house. You'll have to ask my father. He's around back, in the kitchen."

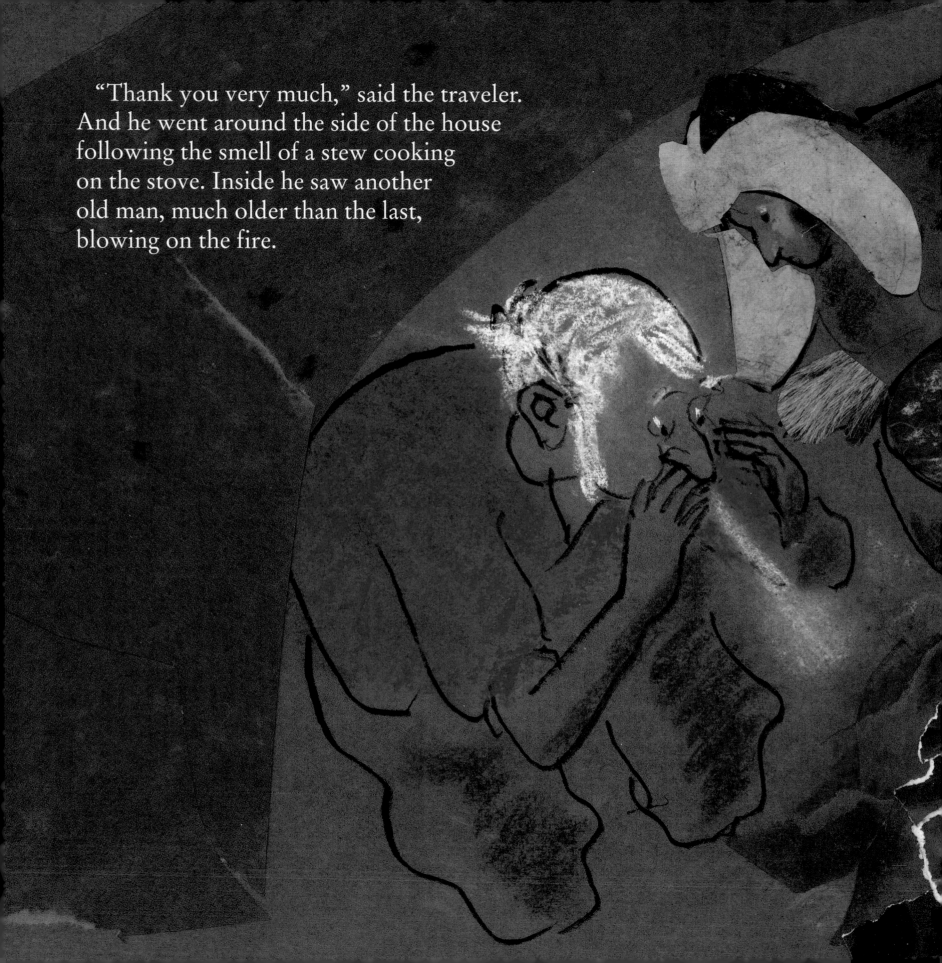

"Thank you very much," said the traveler.
And he went around the side of the house
following the smell of a stew cooking
on the stove. Inside he saw another
old man, much older than the last,
blowing on the fire.

The traveler went in and approached the man saying, "Good evening, Father. Your son sent me to ask you if you would, by any chance, have a room where I could spend the night?"

"Oh," said the old man, looking up with a smile at the hopeful traveler, "I'm not the father of this house. You'll have to ask my father. He's in the parlor."

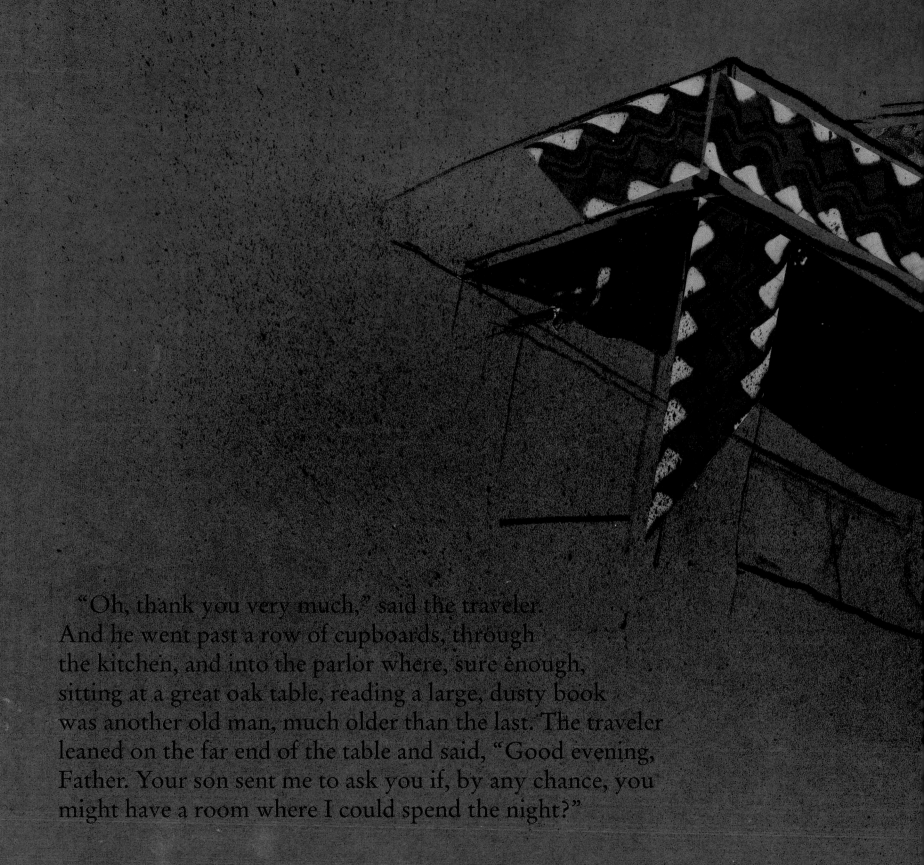

"Oh, thank you very much," said the traveler.
And he went past a row of cupboards, through
the kitchen, and into the parlor where, sure enough,
sitting at a great oak table, reading a large, dusty book
was another old man, much older than the last. The traveler
leaned on the far end of the table and said, "Good evening,
Father. Your son sent me to ask you if, by any chance, you
might have a room where I could spend the night?"

"Eh?"

The traveler raised his voice to a shout. "Would you, by any chance, have a room where I can spend the night?"

"Oh," stuttered the old man, "I am not the father of this house. You'll have to ask my father. He's sitting over there by the hearth."

The traveler looked and there,
sure enough, sitting by the side
of the fire was another old man.
He was trying to smoke his
pipe. Yes, I say trying
because he was so frail
and shaky that every
time he tried to put it
in his mouth
he missed!

The traveler approached the old man
and spoke in a very loud voice so he would
be sure to be heard. "Good evening!"
The old man shrieked and scrunched up his
eyes. "There's no need to shout!"

"Good evening, Father," said the traveler, lowering his voice. "Would you, by any chance, have a room where I could spend the night? I'm cold. I'm wet. I'm weary. I've been walking for hours. Please, anywhere will do."

"Well," said the old man in a very shaky voice, "I'm not the father of this house. You'll have to ask my father." He raised his old, bony finger and pointed. "He's, ah, sleeping, in the bedroom at the far end of the hall."

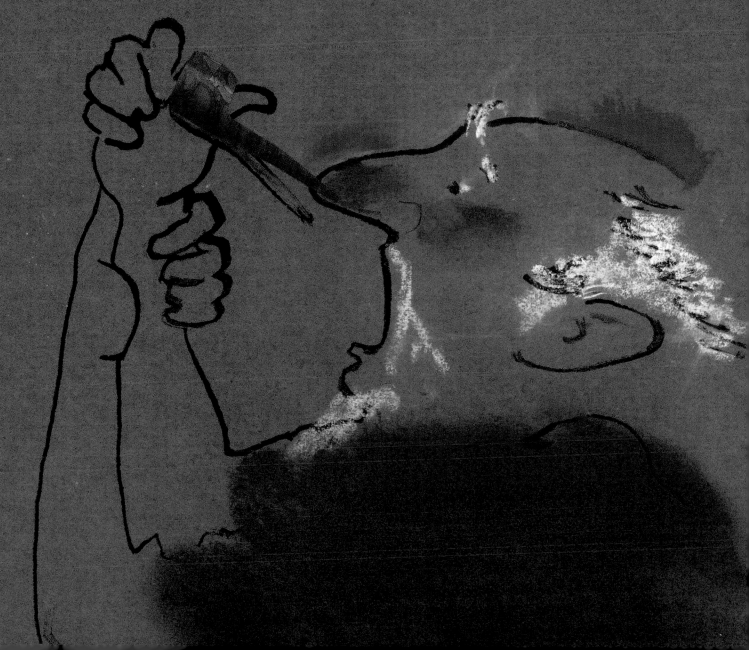

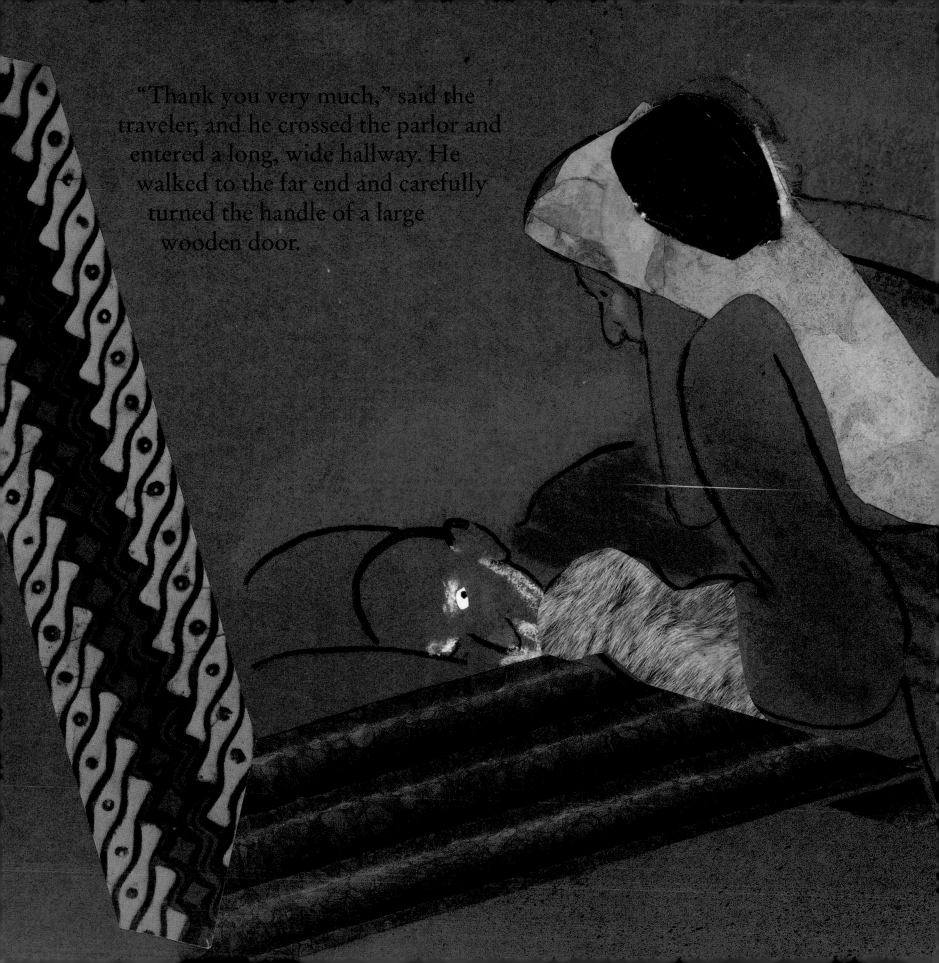

"Thank you very much," said the traveler, and he crossed the parlor and entered a long, wide hallway. He walked to the far end and carefully turned the handle of a large wooden door.

Inside the dimly lit room, he stepped toward a stately bed where he saw a very, very, very, very, very, very old man. His head was small and shrunken with just a wisp of white hair on the pillow, and he lay there motionless under a thick quilt, fast asleep! The traveler waited a long, long time, but at last one of the old man's eyes shot open! The traveler hesitated, and then he whispered, "I'm very sorry to disturb you, Father, but would you, by any chance, have a room where I could spend the night?"

He eagerly turned his head so his ear was close to the old man's face, and he heard a creaky, squeaky voice say, "I'm not the father of this house. You'll have to ask my father. He's lying in the cradle over there."

"Lying in the cradle?" asked the traveler as his brow fell and his heart sank.

"Yes."

The traveler turned and looked and, sure enough, at the foot of the bed he saw a cradle. He took a few tiny steps, bent over, and saw inside a very, very, very, very, very, very, very, very, very old man, so small, so shrunken, he was no bigger than a baby! He moved closer to the cradle and pleaded, very softly and gently, "Good evening, Father. Would you, by any chance, have a room where I could spend the night?"

The traveler closed his eyes and listened for a reply, but all he could hear was a gurgling noise that fluttered and quivered and shook until finally he was able to make out some faint words: "I'm not the father of this house. You'll have to ask my father. He lives on the horn in the hall."

"He lives on the horn in the hall?!" The traveler's
eyes rolled and his stomach rose into his throat.
"Yes."
    The traveler went out into the hall and saw a
magnificent drinking horn at the other end of the
corridor, hanging above two matched doors. He
walked closer and stared up at the horn, but
he could see nothing.

He was just about to give up and go out and lie
down in the cold, wet snow when his eyes happened
to catch a spark of light on the very tip of the horn.
Curious and desperate, he placed a chair on top of a
nearby table, then climbed up and stood on his toes
until his face was level with the tip of the horn.

On the tip of the horn he saw a little speck of dust.
In the center of the speck of dust he saw a little white
pillow. In the middle of the little white pillow were two
little, black, shiny dots. On close inspection, he could
make out that those little, black, shiny dots were two
very small eyes! And the traveler said, very carefully,
for he didn't want to blow away the speck of dust,
"Good evening, Father. Would you, by any chance,
have a room where I could spend the night?"

And he listened, and he listened, and he
listened. And at last he heard a voice as tiny
as a titmouse say, "Yes, my son."

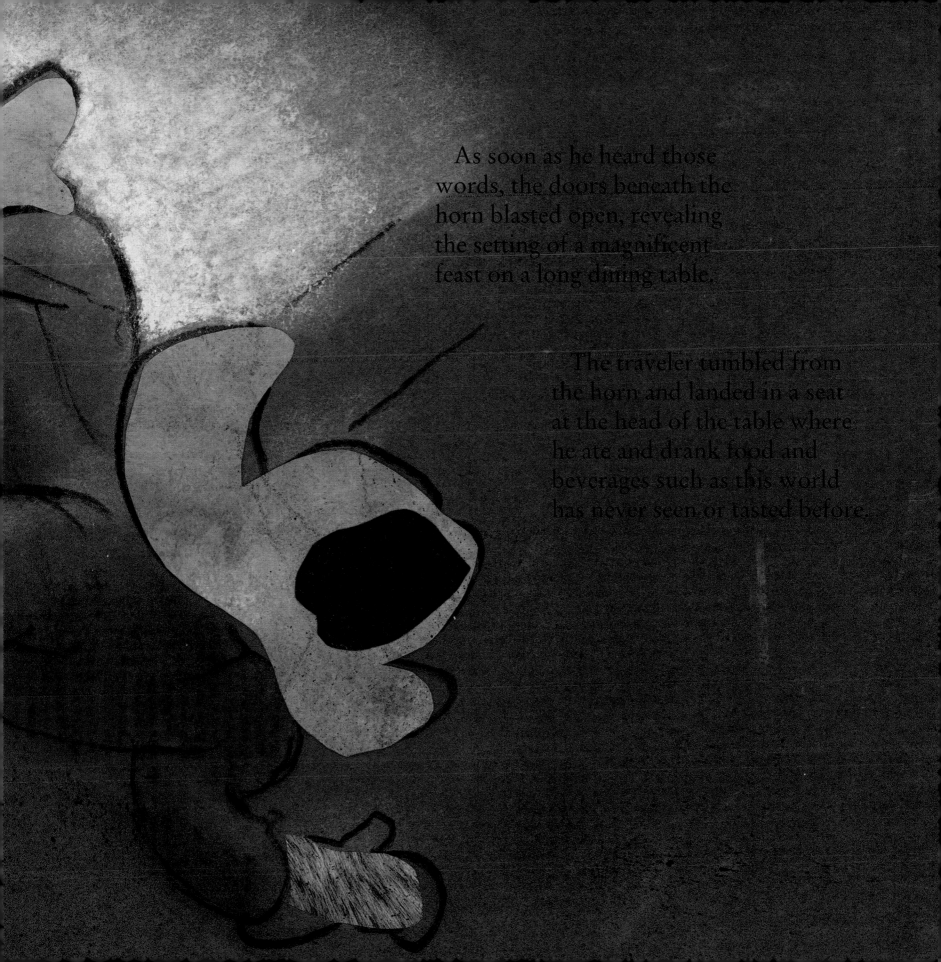

As soon as he heard those words, the doors beneath the horn blasted open, revealing the setting of a magnificent feast on a long dining table.

The traveler tumbled from the horn and landed in a seat at the head of the table where he ate and drank food and beverages such as this world has never seen or tasted before.

The seven fathers of that house stood around the table, each now the size and age of the traveler himself and each wearing a crown upon his head. They watched as the hungry traveler ate and drank until he was full. And then, one by one, they took off their crowns, approached the feasting traveler, and laid them at his feet.

The food was whisked away as if by invisible hands, and a gracious bed, covered in reindeer hide, swept into the room. The traveler fell down on that bed. He was so exhausted. But before he went to sleep, he said another prayer of thanks that he had, at last, found the true father of that house.

And what happened when he woke the next morning? Well, that is another story.

In the storytelling tradition we often say, "Behind me is the one I heard this story from, . . . and behind that storyteller the one who told them the tale," . . . and so on. Amongst the first peoples there was always a profound sense of how we are all connected to the ones who came before us and the spiritual origins that underpin our entire existence. This story was first collected by the great folklorists Asbøjrnsen and Moe, who heard it from one of their Norwegian countrymen, and it is in this spirit that we pass it on to you.

Ashley Ramsden

It was Ashley's telling of *Seven Fathers* on tape that first found its way to my ears in 1998 at my friend George Levenson's house in Santa Cruz, California. We were, at the time, working on a film called *Sadako and a Thousand Paper Cranes*.

I was intrigued by this uniquely Nordic version of a spiritual quest and enjoyed Ashley's very animated telling.

At the time, however, no one thought it was ideal children's book material, even though I've always maintained that children are perfectly capable of comprehending much deeper thoughts and feelings than we are willing to acknowledge.

I was pleased to find this sentiment shared by Neal Porter at Roaring Brook. Thus, this story has found its place in children's literature. Even though George has since passed away, his dream and my appreciation of our friendship have come to a closure by the completion of this book.

Ed Young